Illustrated by the Disney Storybook Artists
Story adapted by Amy Adair

© Disney Enterprises, Inc.

Published by
Louis Weber, C.E.O.
Publications International, Ltd.
7373 North Cicero Avenue
Lincolnwood, Illinois 60712

www.pilbooks.com

Manufactured in China.

8 7 6 5 4 3 2 1

ISBN: 0-7853-9775-2

L ong ago a lamp changed the life of a poor boy and a
princess. The lamp did not seem like it was worth
much. But worth is not what is on the outside, but what is
on the inside. The tale begins on a dark night.

Jafar, the Sultan's crafty advisor, met a thief named
Gazeem. Jafar was greedy. He wanted power. Gazeem
handed Jafar two pieces of a golden scarab. It was exactly
what Jafar had been looking for. He put the two pieces of
the scarab together.

The scarab buzzed and hummed. Then it darted across
the desert, leaving a sparkly trail behind it.

Like magic, a gigantic cave emerged from the sand. It was the Cave of Wonders.

Inside the Cave of Wonders was a magic lamp. Gazeem was supposed to find the lamp for Jafar.

Gazeem slowly stepped into the mouth of the Cave.

"Only one can enter here!" the Cave roared. "He must be a Diamond in the Rough."

Suddenly the earth trembled, and the Cave of Wonders disappeared in the sand.

"I can't believe it," said Iago, Jafar's parrot. "We will never get that lamp!"

"Patience," said Jafar. "We will find this Diamond in the Rough."

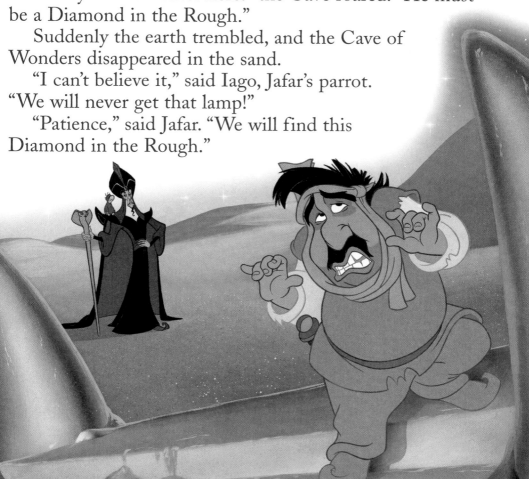

Aladdin, a young man in the city, was hungry. He and his best friend, a monkey named Abu, went to the market to steal a loaf of bread. Aladdin never had money for food. He and Abu stole fruit and bread every day.

Aladdin stared at the palace in the distance. He wished he lived there. Then all of his problems would be solved, he thought.

Princess Jasmine was supposed to find a husband before her next birthday. Many princes had traveled from faraway kingdoms to try to win her heart.

Princess Jasmine had found something wrong with every single one of them.

"You are a princess," said her father, the Sultan. "The law says that you must marry a prince."

"But Father," Jasmine said. "I want to marry for love."

That night, Jasmine dressed like a peasant and climbed the palace wall. Rajah, her tiger, bit the hem of her dress. He did not want her to leave.

"I'm sorry, Rajah," Jasmine whispered. "I cannot stay here and have my life lived for me."

Rajah understood. He gently helped her over the wall.

Jasmine made her way to the city market. She had never seen so many people or things.

"Buy a pot," someone yelled.

"Fresh fish," another called.

Aladdin watched the young woman. He knew she was special.

Jasmine saw a poor little boy and a girl. She thought they looked hungry, so she handed one of them a piece of fruit from a nearby stand.

"You'd better be able to pay for that," a man said as he grabbed Jasmine's arm. But Jasmine didn't have any money. Suddenly, Aladdin and Abu jumped in front of her.

Abu stole another apple off the man's stand and tossed it to Aladdin.

"I've been looking all over for you," he told Jasmine as he winked.

"She is my sister," Aladdin told the man. He handed him the apple that Abu had stolen. The man thought it was the same apple Jasmine had taken.

Aladdin took Jasmine to his home. It wasn't fancy, but it had a view of the palace.

"I wonder what it would be like to live there," Aladdin said, pointing to the palace.

Jasmine sat down. "You would never be free to make your own choices."

Suddenly, the Sultan's guards stormed into Aladdin's house. Aladdin and Jasmine ran to an open window, and Aladdin held out his hand for Jasmine. "Do you trust me?" Aladdin asked Jasmine.

Jasmine nodded. They quickly leaped out the window and landed safely on the ground. But more guards were waiting for them. The guards arrested Aladdin.

"Unhand him, by order of the princess," Jasmine said, revealing her headband with a blue diamond in the center.

"I am sorry, Princess," a guard said. "But my orders come from Jafar." The guards took Aladdin to the palace's dark dungeon.

Jafar had been watching Aladdin. He was sure Aladdin was the Diamond in the Rough he had been searching for. He hoped Aladdin could enter the Cave of Wonders and find the magic lamp.

Jafar disguised himself as an old prisoner. "I need a strong man to find the lamp that is hidden in the Cave of Wonders," Jafar told Aladdin. "If you find it, you will be rewarded with treasures."

"There is one problem," Aladdin said. "We are locked in down here."

"Things aren't always what they seem," Jafar said as he opened a hidden door that led to the desert.

Jafar, Aladdin, and Abu soon arrived at the cave. "Who disturbs my slumber?" the Cave roared.

"It is I," Aladdin said.

"Proceed. Touch nothing but the lamp," the Cave warned.

Aladdin slowly stepped into the Cave. He went down hundreds of winding steps and saw piles of shimmery gold.

Suddenly a carpet started to move. It was a Magic Carpet. It led Aladdin right to the magic lamp. But while Aladdin was getting the lamp, Abu spotted a beautiful ruby. He reached out to take it.

"You have touched the forbidden treasure!" the Cave bellowed as it started to crumble.

Aladdin and Abu climbed onto the Magic Carpet and flew through the passageways.

Kaboom! All the gold exploded and started to melt. It popped and bubbled like hot lava.

Aladdin made it to the mouth of the Cave just in time. Abu hopped out of the Cave to safety. Aladdin reached for Jafar's hand.

"Give me the lamp first," Jafar ordered.

Aladdin handed it to him. But Jafar did not help him out of the Cave. Instead, he pushed Aladdin back in. Abu jumped in after Aladdin, but not before Abu grabbed the magic lamp away from Jafar.

There was no way out of the cave. Aladdin looked at the lamp that Abu had stolen from Jafar.

"It looks like a worthless piece of junk. There seems to be something written here, but it is hard to make out," Aladdin said, rubbing the side of the lamp.

Boom! Boom! Boom! Colorful fireworks burst out of the lamp. Then a big blue genie floated out.

The Genie looked at Aladdin and spoke in a deep voice. "What can I do for you, master?"

Aladdin was stunned. "I'm your master?" he stammered.

"You are the boss," the Genie said. "Tell me what you wish and it is yours!"

The Genie explained that he would grant Aladdin any three wishes.

Aladdin could wish for anything in the world — except more wishes or love.

Aladdin thought for a moment. He wished he wasn't stuck in the Cave of Wonders. But he didn't want to waste one of his wishes on getting out. So he tricked the Genie.

"You probably can't even get us out of this Cave," Aladdin said slyly.

"Yes I can," the Genie said. "Hop on the Magic Carpet. We're outta here!"

Once they were safely out of the Cave, Aladdin did not know what to wish for first.

"What would you wish for?" Aladdin asked his new friend the Genie.

"I'd wish for freedom," said the Genie. "I have cosmic powers, but I have an itty-bitty living space."

The Genie sank back into the magic lamp. The Genie told Aladdin that freedom would be better than all the treasures in the world. But the only way that the Genie could ever be free was if his master wished him free. Aladdin felt bad for the Genie. He promised that he would use his final wish to set the Genie free.

Aladdin thought about his two other wishes. He remembered Jasmine. He knew the law stated that she had to marry a prince. And he certainly was no prince.

"Genie," Aladdin said, "I wish for you to make me a real prince!"

Poof! Aladdin was now a prince. Then the Genie turned Abu into a gigantic elephant. He thought it would impress the princess.

Aladdin rode Abu through the city. "Make way for Prince Ali Ababwa!" people shouted.

Jasmine was not impressed. She was sure he was just another boring prince.

That night, Aladdin floated up to Jasmine's
room on the Magic Carpet. Jasmine was sure he
was the same boy she had met in the
marketplace. Aladdin wanted her to
think he was a real prince.

"Do you trust me?" Aladdin
asked Jasmine, just like he had done
in the marketplace. Jasmine nodded.

Aladdin helped her onto the Magic
Carpet. They flew all over the world.
They floated through fluffy clouds, soared
with geese, and saw hundreds of
stars that sparkled like
diamonds. "It's so magical,"
Jasmine said. "It's a shame
Abu had to miss this."

"He doesn't really like to fly," Aladdin said. He suddenly realized he had given away his true identity.

"You are the boy from the market," Jasmine said. "Did you think I wouldn't figure it out?"

Aladdin lied again. He told Jasmine that sometimes he dressed like a commoner to escape the pressures of palace life. Before long, Aladdin and Jasmine floated back to the castle on the flying carpet.

"Good night, my handsome prince," Jasmine said.

"Good night, my princess," Aladdin said.

Princess Jasmine felt wonderful. She knew she had finally found her prince.

Jafar thought the only way he could become the Sultan was to marry Jasmine. So he ordered his guards to throw Aladdin into the ocean.

As Aladdin sank to the bottom, his hand rubbed the magic lamp. The Genie saved his friend's life.

When Aladdin returned to the palace, Jafar stole the magic lamp. He rubbed it and wished to become the Sultan. The Genie was forced to grant his wish. Jafar made Princess Jasmine and her father his servants.

Jafar wanted even more power. His second wish was to become a sorcerer. Aladdin knew he had to save Jasmine and her father. So he tricked Jafar.

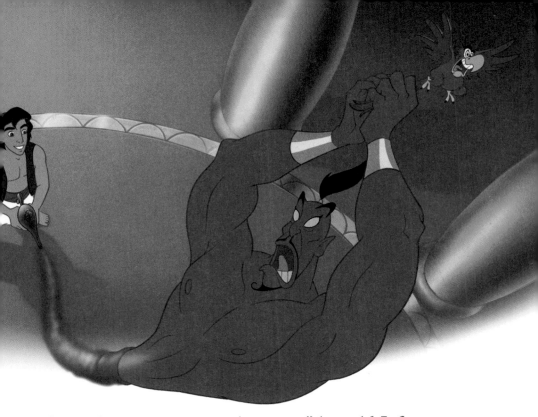

"Genie has more power than you," he told Jafar.

Jafar thought for a moment. Then he used his final wish. "I wish to be an all-powerful genie!" Jafar said.

The Genie covered his eyes and pointed his finger. Jafar turned into a gigantic genie.

"You want to be a genie," Aladdin yelled, opening the lid to the magic lap. "You've got it and everything that goes with it. You have phenomenal cosmic powers and an itty-bitty living space."

Jafar was sucked into the lamp. Even his parrot, Iago, disappeared. The kingdom was safe again.

Aladdin turned to Jasmine. "I'm sorry I lied to you about being a prince," he said.

"You have one wish left," the Genie said. "Say the word and you are a prince again."

Aladdin did not want to pretend anymore. He wanted to keep his promise to the Genie. So with his final wish, Aladdin wished for the Genie's freedom.

"You have proven your worth to me," Jasmine's father said to Aladdin. "From this day forward the princess can choose whomever she wants to marry."

"I choose Aladdin!" Jasmine said. Princess Jasmine's wish had finally come true.